This spooky sticker activity book belongs to:

....

Add some
Halloween stickers
to the night sky!

This witch is missing her friend. Stick a black cat on her broomstick!

Count the pumpkins in the pumpkin patch.
Use the stickers to give them funny faces.

Answer: 6 pumpkins

Mommy and Daddy Bat are sleeping upside down in the tree. Add a baby bat sticker to make the family complete.

Can you draw a silly spider
in this big web?

Color in this picture, then draw some scary faces in the picture frames!

Use the stickers to invent
your own potion.
Which ingredients will you choose?

Wendy Witch's mice
have escaped!
How many do you see?

Draw the other half of Wendy Witch's pets!

Trace the dotted lines to
complete the pumpkin and bat.
Then color them in.

Who has made each spooky shadow?
Find the stickers that match each shape.

Use star stickers to decorate this little wizard's hat and cape.

Color these pages to complete the cats' Halloween party!

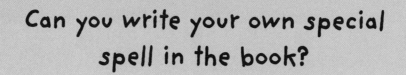
Can you write your own special
spell in the book?

The wizards' wands are all mixed up! Follow the lines to see which wand belongs to each wizard.

The skeletons are dancing!
Use the stickers to fill in their
missing bones.

Can you find five differences between these hungry baby dragons?

Wendy Witch is building a gingerbread house. Use the stickers to help her decorate it with sweet treats.

What has gotten tangled in the mummy's bandages?
Look for the right stickers to find out!

Find the pets' hats on the sticker pages to complete their costumes.

Use your imagination and crayons to turn these shapes into spooky characters.

Mommy ghost has lost her baby ghosts. Can you lead her though the maze to help her find them?

Draw a spooky ghost
in the archway.

Answer:

Color this picture of a hungry monster who's about to gobble some cupcakes!

Color in the haunted house. Can you draw some bats in the sky?